The
Three
Little
Pigs

Modern Curriculum Press
**BEGINNING
TO
READ**
Series

Margaret Hillert

The
Three
Little
Pigs

illustrated by Irma Wilde

MODERN CURRICULUM PRESS
Cleveland • Toronto

Copyright © 1963, by Modern Curriculum Press, Inc. Original copyright © 1963, by Follett Publishing Company, a division of Follett Corporation. All rights reserved. No part of this book may be reproduced in any form without written permission from the publisher. Manufactured in the United States of America.

ISBN 0-8136-5535-8 (paperback)
ISBN 0-8136-5035-6 (hardbound)

4 5 6 7 8 9   96 95 94

6

Here is a pig.

Here is a pig.

And here is a pig.

One, two, three.

Three little pigs.

Three funny little pigs.

See my house.

It is a little house.

It is yellow.

Little pig, little pig.

I want to come in.

You can not.

You can not.

You can not come in.

I can puff the house down.

Puff, puff, puff.

Here is my house.

It is a funny little house.

Little pig, little pig.

I want to come in.

You can not.

You can not.

You can not come in.

See me puff, puff, puff.

I can puff the house down.

Look here, look here.

My house is a big one.

It is red.

Little pig, little pig.

I want to come in.

Go away.

Go away.

You can not come in.

See me puff.

I can puff.

I can puff the house down.

See here, see here.

My house is not down.

I can go up, up, up.

I can go in.

Oh my, oh my.

It is funny.

You can not go up.

You can not come down.

And you can not come in.

Modern Curriculum Press Beginning-To-Read Books

Margaret Hillert, author of several books in the MCP Beginning-To-Read Series, is a writer, poet, and teacher.

The Three Little Pigs

The classic nursery story told in just 34 preprimer words with charming illustrations that carry the action of the story.

Word List

7	here		house	15	puff
	is		it		the
	a		yellow		down
	pig				
				19	me
9	and	13	I		
			want	20	look
10	one		to		big
	two		come		red
	three		in		
	little			22	go
	funny				away
		14	you		
12	see		can	25	up
	my		not	26	oh